What Shall I Dream About?

by Becky De Oliveira
illustrated by Chiara Vercesi

'Mama,' the boy asks,
'what shall I dream about?'

The wind is howling outside his window. Snow is falling. The rough branch of a tree scrapes the bricks of the house. The boy is wrapped in a soft duvet with a sailboat pattern. He is hugging a teddy bear dressed in pyjamas and dinosaur slippers. The boy yawns and rubs his eyes.

'Hmmm,' his mother says, closing her eyes to think. 'That's a tough one. There are so many beautiful things to dream about.' She strokes his hair. 'How about . . .

. . . picking small, sweet cherries in the warm sunlight?

. . . warm, red mittens on a cold, snowy day?

. . . *floating on your back in a big green pond?*

. . . spinning circles on roller skates?

. . . jumping in piles of crisp autumn leaves?

. . . a cave filled with smooth pebbles?

. . . tiptoeing through a field of tall green ferns?

. . . guinea pigs nibbling your fingers?

. . . sleeping in a frosty white igloo?

... *licking an enormous, round rainbow lolly?*

. . . curling up on a thick sheepskin rug?

. . . bouncing on a trampoline at night under a big round moon?

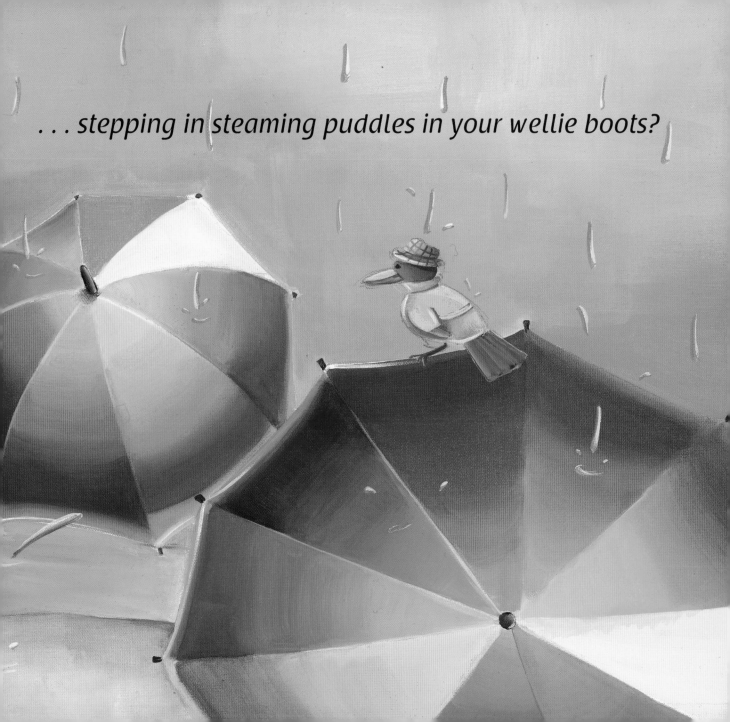

. . . stepping in steaming puddles in your wellie boots?

. . . sliding into a pit of soft, pink cotton balls?

*. . . standing knee-deep in a stream,
catching tiny green frogs?*

. . . *gently swinging in a hammock?*

. . . throwing hunks of bread to a drift of swans?

. . . The boy's eyes are half-closed.
'Mmmm,' he says. 'Those are good ones.'

'I saved the best for last,' the mother says softly, tucking the duvet around his chin. 'Dream about the face of Jesus. Dream that he's looking down on you while you sleep. He's smiling because he's proud of everything you are.'

The mother kisses the sleeping boy's head and switches off the light.

Saying thank you to God

by KAREN HOLFORD

This beautifully written and illustrated story
on stewardship will delight young children.
It also includes practical activities and
suggestions that will encourage children
to want to say *thank you to God*.

Also published by Autumn House

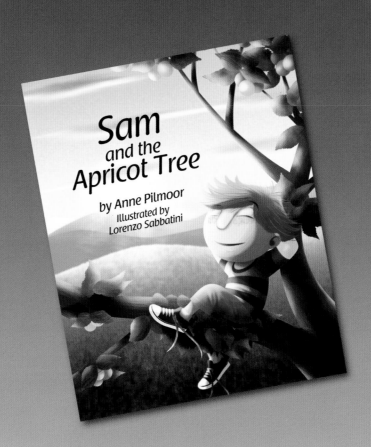

This beautifully illustrated book is a story about Sam who pretends one of the branches in the apricot tree is a horse. He rides it like a cowboy and the inevitable happens. Find out how he tries to 'fix' the tree and what he learns about forgiveness.

Also published by Autumn House

Your Angel

by Becky De Oliveira
Illustrated by Alice De Marco

Children will enjoy the stories and beautiful illustrations
about the boy who throws out a series of challenges
to his angel to show him what he looks like.
His mother handles the boy's frustration
in an unusual but remarkable way. . . .
This is sure to become a child's favourite book.

Also published by Autumn House

First published in 2009 • Copyright © 2009 Autumn House Publishing (Europe) Ltd. • Author: Becky De Oliveira • Illustrator: Chiara Varcesi

British Library Cataloguing in Publication Data. A catalogue record for this book is available from the British Library. ISBN 978-1-906381-66-0

Published by Autumn House, Alma Park, Grantham, Lincs. Printed in Thailand